Fox & Goose on the loose!

Written by: Angel Evenson

DEDICATION

To my beautiful family that is always up for an adventure.

ACKNOWLEDGMENTS

To my husband, Eric who always supports my dreams.

To my best friends Vanessa & Beth that always make me feel like I can fly.

To my kids who always inspire me to be better every day.

To my Lord and Savior, Jesus Christ

Fox & Goose are on the loose…where are they going?

There never was a place they didn't want to go

Riding airplanes, boats and cars to and fro.

Not meant for cages they'd escape when they could,

chasing what their adventure seeking hearts thought they should.

One day Goose said...

"I'm tired of the snow on my little webbed toes.

I want to go where the sunshine goes!"

Fox got excited and shared with delight

"Yes! That's a great idea! Let's go tonight!"

Silly little Fox got right to packing.

Toy trucks, swim trunks and some food for snacking.

Responsible Goose grabbed her toothbrush, sunglasses, and her yoga mat for those sunset beach classes.

Fox never planned, he just enjoyed the ride.

Goose loved adventure with him by her side.

Flying all day was a simple task for Goose,

but Fox always ended up being the caboose.

So, Goose made a backpack to carry her friend,

Where he could ride with her safely to the end.

It was almost 7o'clock, so Goose told Fox what to do.

"Climb on my back!"

and

away

they

flew!

Fox fell asleep almost right away,

and Goose just smiled because it was easier this way.

No questions, no whining, no "are we there yet?!",

just a peaceful flight traveling as quick as a jet.

As the sun started rising and the clouds disappeared

Fox blinked open his eyes and thought, this is weird.

"Where are we Goose?

I slept all night long. You said when I woke up, we'd be there...

You were wrong."

"Patience my friend, we are almost there.

The sun is shining, you'll see it soon, I swear."

Right at that moment

the sun warmed their faces.

As Goose slowed her flapping

they soared down to new places.

"I see it! There it is!" yelled Fox so elated.

A beautiful moment they both long had awaited.

The sand came quickly as Goose landed softly.

She gently nudged Fox,

"now you can get off me."

Goose waddled in the sand as Fox ran like crazy.

She stretched and said "NOW I can be lazy!"

She dipped her webbed toes in the cool ocean tide.

As Fox out of nowhere showed up by her side.

"Is it everything you hoped it would be?

This adventure you chose to seek with me?

Fox asked very inquisitively.

The location was different,

but the love was the same.

So, they shared that love,

because, after all, that's really why they came.

ABOUT THE AUTHOR

Angel Evenson is a passionate storyteller that loves adventure. As a Wife and Mother, she has found her writing inspiration through all of the curve balls life throws at her. Believing that though you cannot control what happens to you in life, there is always something you can learn from it; she is committed to teaching children the same mindset. Her mission is to create positive stories that share life changing lessons.

Made in United States
Troutdale, OR
12/09/2024